The All Africa Wildlife Express

For Gabriel and Mo

First published in 2017 by Tafelberg,
an imprint of NB Publishers,
a division of Media24 Boeke (Pty) Ltd,
40 Heerengracht, Cape Town
Text © 2017 Rosamund Haden
Illustrations © 2017 Tony Pinchuck
Cover and book design by Tony Pinchuck
Printed and bound in Malaysia by Times Offset
First edition, first impression 2017

ISBN: 978-0-624-08130-2

The All Africa Wildlife Express

Story by Rosamund Haden

Pictures by Tony Pinchuck

TAFELBERG

A postcard blew down on the tropical breeze
And landed near elephant's large wrinkly knees.

Inviting all animals tall, short and wide
To a wild monkey party with mad monkey rides.
A steam train was waiting to whisk them away
To the Hotel Splendide on Coconut Bay.

PLEASE join us

For fun, games and monkey busines

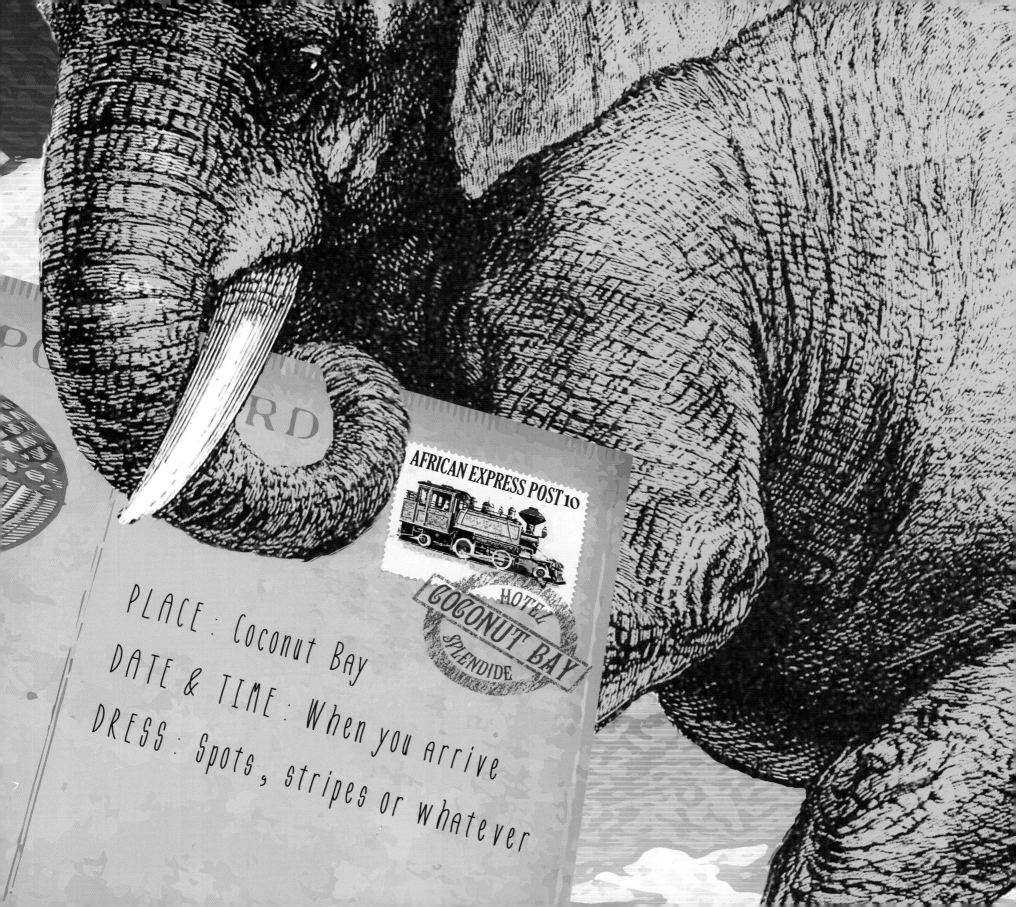

PLACE: Coconut Bay

DATE & TIME: When you arrive

DRESS: Spots, stripes or whatever

AFRICAN EXPRESS POST 10

HOTEL COCONUT BAY SPLENDIDE

At each jungle station and every bush stop

Elephant tooted aloud and a lot.

Calling all animals onto the train

As it steamed through the jungle in sunshine and rain.

All Africa
Wildlife Express

Animals queued at the red station gate,
Baboon gave out tickets which monkey then ate.

The best thing of all was playing I spy
Under the endless blue African sky.

The adventure was wild and crazy and far
But really much better than going by car.

At last they arrived for their party play date
At the Hotel Splendide's majestical gate.

The monkeys were waiting with welcome balloons
And from the hotel floated magical tunes.

As the majestical gate opened wide

They jumped off the train and all rushed inside.

And on the hotel's immaculate lawn
The animals partied from dusk until dawn.
Lion told leopard he'd look really cool
If he jumped out the window and into the pool.

Hippo, wild dog and cheetah had tea
Under the shade of the lala palm tree.

Hotel Splendide

Gnu went ballooning and monkey did tricks
Anteater gobbled some rock candy sticks.

Bushbabies slid down the wild water slide
Giraffe and some friends rode the carousel rides.

After the party and back on the train

They promised the monkeys they'd soon come again.